THE ANIMAL

By David Kherdian and Nonny Hogrogian

ALFRED A. KNOPF, NEW YORK

THIS IS A BORZOI BOOK PUBLISHED BY ALFRED A. KNOPF, INC.

Copyright © 1984 by David Kherdian

Illustrations Copyright © 1984 by Nonny H. Kherdian

All rights reserved under International and Pan-American
Copyright Conventions. Published in the United States
by Alfred A. Knopf, Inc., New York, and simultaneously in
Canada by Random House of Canada Limited, Toronto.
Distributed by Random House, Inc., New York.
Manufactured in the United States of America
1 3 5 7 9 0 8 6 4 2

Library of Congress Cataloging in Publication Data
Kherdian, David. The animal.   Summary: A newcomer's enthusiasm for
everything causes the animals to speculate on the nature of perception.
[1. Animals—Fiction.   2. Perception—Fiction]
I. Hogrogian, Nonny, ill.   II. Title.   PZ7.K527An   1984   [E]   83-22268
ISBN 0-394-85597-3   ISBN 0-394-95597-8 (lib. bdg.)

For Adra

They were eating their carrots.
The animal was smiling.
He was smiling and staring at Elephant's trunk.
"He loves it," Goose said.

The animal finished his carrot
and smiled at the flower.
"What is he doing?" Crocodile asked.
"Maybe he's getting ready to eat it,"
Goose said.

The animal put the flower in his hair.
"Maybe he thinks it's a bow," Lion said.
"Either that or he loves it," Fox said.
They all laughed. The animal laughed too.
Everybody but Crocodile
put flowers on their heads.
Crocodile put his between his teeth
and made a face.

The animal crouched and stared
at a dandelion puff. The others
gathered around him.
"Will he eat it?" Ostrich asked.
"Or does he love it?"
"Who would love that?" Lion exclaimed.
"The animal does," Elephant answered.

Fox picked the dandelion for the animal
and then blew on it,
scattering the little parachute-like puffs
into the air.

The animal ran after the puffs
and disappeared over the hills.
It wasn't long before he reappeared,
smiling and chasing a butterfly.

"I think the animal loves everything," said Fox.
"Why?" Goose asked.
"Do you think it's because he's new here
and seeing things for the first time?" asked Fox.
The animal was smiling up at a cloud.
"Well, I don't always love everything
the first time I see it," Lion said.

"Then maybe it's because
you haven't *seen* it," Elephant replied.
"Sure I have," Lion answered.
"What is seeing?" Goose asked.
"I know," Crocodile said, "it's looking."
Elephant shook his head.
"But how can you look without seeing?" Lion asked.

"Well," Elephant said, "when you look
at that tree, what do you see?"
"I see a big brown trunk," Lion said,
"and branches with many green leaves."
"But that's looking, not seeing," Elephant said.

The animal was smiling at the tree.
"What does the animal see
when he looks at the tree?" Lion asked.
"He sees the same tree we see," Elephant said,
"but he also sees the life in the tree.
The animal knows the tree.
It's like . . . well,
like seeing a friend."

"And what happens?" Goose asked.
"He loves it," Elephant said,
and they all laughed.

"Seeing is loving," Elephant said.
"Oh!" said Lion. "Seeing is loving."

They all looked at the animal again.
He was watching a bird.
"He loves it," Ostrich said.
"He loves it," Crocodile and Elephant said.

"He loves it," Goose and Fox said.
"He loves it," Lion said.

"I love it," the animal said.